Clint Faraday
book forty eight
Dead in the Water

A ship sitting outside the harbor at Chiriqui Grande. It's been there two days and no sign of life. Naldo says it seems to just be dead in the water.

The captain was.

Contents

About the author

CD Moulton has traveled extensively over much of the world both in the music business, where he was a rock guitarist, songwriter and arranger and in an import/export business. He has been everything from a bar owner to auto salvage (junkyard) manager, longshoreman to high steel worker, orchid grower to landscaper, tropical fish farmer to commercial fisherman. He started writing books in 1983 and has published more than 350 books as of January 1, 2023. His most popular books to date are about research with orchids, though much of his science fiction and fantasy work has proven popular. He wrote the CD Grimes, PI series, and the Det. Nick Storie series, Clint Faraday series, and many other works.

He now resides in Gualaca, Chiriqui, Panamá, where he writes books, plays music with friends, does research with orchids and medicinal plants. He has lately become involved in fighting for the rights of the indigenous people, who are among his closest friends, and in fighting the extreme corruption in the courts and police in Panamá.

He offers the free e-book, *Fading Paradise*, that explains what he has been through because of the corruption.

CD is the discoverer of the Chadam Protocol for curing cancer.

Facebook page Ambrosia peruviana for cancer.

"It's been sitting out there for two days," Naldo said to his good friend, Clint Faraday, retired PI from Florida, now living on the comarca Ngobe Bugle in Panamá. He was speaking of a ship sitting just outside of the harbor at Chiriqui Grande. "No one's seen anyone on it. It seems to just be dead in the water. It doesn't move.

"Omar and I went close and called, but there was no response."

"No one came ashore to aduana?"

"I don't think so. Lizeth watches for the aduana and says it was just there when she came on duty at five thirty in the morning. There were no lights. She doesn't know anything about it."

Clint took out his binoculars and looked at the ship. There was no sign anyone was aboard. He got the name and numbers. It didn't seem to be in very good repair.

It was Libyan registration? What was it doing there?

"I'll go to aduana and check out the numbers," Clint promised. "It's not registered in this country. You'd think the US Coast Guard ship would check it out."

"It's in Panamanian waters. They can't check that close."

Clint nodded. Naldo said Omar was waiting. They had to get back to their fishing. They were getting conch and octopus for the market. They had a big order to fill.

Clint tied his boat securely and went across to the aduana. Lizeth checked the numbers and said it wasn't ever registered as being in Panamanian waters. She called the US Coast Guard and they hadn't checked it. It wasn't even noted as having come into Panamanian waters. That was very strange in itself. They checked everything!

The coast guard ship's communications officer checked international. The ship wasn't registered. Anywhere. There were no such numbers on record, meaning it was probably a drug runner.

"Not even maybe!" Clint said. "It's too big for that. It's 'way too slow in the water. Something's definitely not...."

The radio came on with an attention call. It was the coast guard man.

"Lizeth? That ship was listed as missing at sea thirty six years ago! It was last heard of near the Devil's Triangle! They sent a search and rescue, but never found it. They felt it would be out of fuel or had engine failure, but it had disappeared.

One ship a few miles more north said they had it on radar for awhile, but there was no distress call. It hasn't been recorded as having been seen anywhere! The captain and crew never were heard of again!"

"Oh, shit!" Clint cried. "I have to get to that ship! I don't think I want to go aboard that thing, but someone will have to!"

"We'll take the launch. It's my responsibility to check it, anyhow.

"This is scary!"

They went to the aduana launch. Lizeth called an officer to take care of the office until she returned. She took an automatic from the rack. Clint asked why.

"Too many horror movies. I half expect some drooling monster to be aboard that thing! I don't want to be aboard when it shifts into another dimension.

"I'm glad that's not real!"

Clint thought for a minute as they went toward the ship. He used his cellular to call Dave, his author friend. Dave had studied that kind of thing to use in his science fiction books.

They were just off the starboard side. Clint told Lizeth to stop out there and wait. Dave finally answered.

"Yo, Clint! Wapping?"

"Dave, this is serious, but it's not going to sound like it is.

"We have a ship sitting about fifteen meters from us. It's an old ship that's Libyan registered. It disappeared in the Devil's Triangle thirty six years ago and hasn't been seen or heard of since. The captain and crew were never seen again. It was just sitting here, dead in the water, two days ago when Lizeth came on duty. It wasn't seen coming by the coast guard ship. It looks deserted to me. No lights, rusty, no motion aboard.

"I don't know what's going on, but I really don't want to go aboard that thing, even with Lizeth's A-K forty seven!

"Is there anything to dimensional shift or any of that stuff?"

"It would take a hell of a lot of power, but it's theoretically possible. Some very strange things have happened in the Devil's Triangle. It could have a nexal transfer point that moves through at times, but that's tabloid science.

"I'm in Darien! I wish I could be there to see it!

"Okay. I have this thing on record. Go aboard and describe everything. Do you have enough battery?"

"I think so. It's fully charged.

"Lizeth, go alongside."

They went to the boarding platform, which was

at the water line, which meant the ship was carrying a load or had taken on water. He called with the megaphone, but there was no sign that anyone was aboard.

He secured the launch and climbed the ladder to the deck. It looked exactly like a ship that had been sitting in drydock for a few years. Accumulations of detritus and rust.

He helped Lizeth aboard. They called, but got no response.

"Dave, we're on the deck. There's some cargo under rotted tarps and there's a lot of seaweed and dirt, plus everything's rusty. Can you record pictures?"

"Yo!"

Clint sent pictures all around. Lizeth went to the port and opened it. She looked inside and said, "Oh, shit! Oh, holy shit!"

Clint went to look in. There were two skeletons laying by the stairs to the control cabin. Clint took pictures and warned that he couldn't send many before the batteries would die.

They went up the ladder to the wheelhouse. There was no one there. Clint noted a few things and took some pictures, then they went to the bunk room. There was nothing there. They went to the cargo hold. It was full of old cargo in boxes and drums. Next the fore cargo hold. Same.

They went down to the engine room. It had a few inches of water in it. It also had a body in a captain's uniform.

"Well, Dave! Those skeletons have been there maybe thirty six years. This one hasn't been here much more than thirty six hours!

"I sent the pictures from the wheelhouse. This ship was under power recently. This man died, from the looks of it, about two or three ago.

"It's still weird!

"I have my camera on my boat. I'll get it and bring Tonio out here. We have one hell of a mystery. Maybe several of them. This ship was somewhere for the past thirty six years! We have to trace back where. We have to find what is or was on this ship. This size, we have to find at least two more skeletons. If they're not here, we have to find where they are. I have a few hard questions for them."

"Hijack. Inside job," Dave suggested. Clint agreed that was a good possibility.

Clint went up to the deck and asked Lizeth to take the launch in, get the camera from his boat and bring Tonio from the police back out with her.

"I have the weapon and there's nothing here now. You go. I'll see that nothing's touched. I'll stay on deck.

"Clint?"

"Yes?"

"That man in the captain's uniform. He looked like he was about eighty years old to me."

"I'd say so."

"Do you think he really was the captain of this ship?"

"I think that's very possible, even probable."

"Do you think he brought it here?"

"Also."

"The others are dead. The skeletons. He's the only one aboard. Could he have brought this ship here alone?"

"It's possible, but I don't think so. We have some very strong evidence he didn't."

"We do?"

"Yes. Such as who killed him if he brought it here alone?"

"Maybe he died of a heart attack or something like that?"

"Not likely. I think he went down to the engine room to try to make it look like something from the tales of the Devil's Triangle."

"Why?"

"To hide what's been happening for thirty five years. He would make it look like the engines were ... I think he was going to jettison any fuel that was still in the tanks. He would make it look like the ship couldn't have been brought here under power and would slip over the side and disappear somewhere here.

"We'll have to find out why. This is a hell of a mystery from any angle!"

Clint tied his boat to the platform. Tonio tied the aduana launch to the other end. They went aboard. Lizeth was waiting. She seemed scared.

"What's the matter?!" Clint cried.

"Nothing. This old thing makes noises. I'm alone on a ship that disappeared thirty six years ago with some skeletons and a dead man. I watch too many movies. What can I tell you? I have an overactive imagination! I heard a baby cry and almost shit in my panties! It was a damned cat! I was a millimeter from shooting the thing!"

"Calm down. We're here now. Clint wants to take pictures of every inch of this boat and use the same time to find whatever there is to find.

"Clint, if you'll take the engine room first, we can get on with our part."

Clint agreed and went to the engine room to carefully take the pictures. He spent twenty minutes and didn't miss an inch. He took special notice of the fuel gages. They were on empty for all tanks. That partly confirmed what Clint thought the captain was doing down there when he was killed.

There was no evidence of fuel being dumped in the area. That changed his ideas a slight bit.

He called Tonio, who came in with Dr. Cortez, the ME. They went to the body. Cortez said the body died between seventy two and sixty eight hours ago, after using several modern testers. Modern science could use breakdown of certain chemicals to very accurately determine time of death when it was in such a location and with the conditions. The temperature didn't vary in that engine room enough to matter. The rate of breakdown was constant, affected only by the loss of body temperature, initially.

They turned the body over. The sewn-on tag said "Capt. Garcia." The uniform was old. Cortez said he'd estimate eighty six to eighty nine. He died from being struck over the head from behind and to the left. One blow. Massive damage that wasn't apparent until the body was turned over.

Clint went to the wheelhouse to repeat with the picture taking there. He found the log and the register. There was a bill of lading and insurance papers. Clint photographed all of them.

The wheel had been used. The dust and dirt were partly scraped off when it was turned. The switches had the dirt and dust wiped off when they were thrown.

Clint thought. The keys were in the ignition. It

was on. There was no charge left in any of the batteries.

No fuel dumped, but the tanks empty. It had been planned to have the ship run out of fuel where it sat. The captain would know to the meter how far he could go on a certain amount of fuel under the conditions. He was in the engine room to discharge the batteries. He had accomplished that when he was killed.

The bunk room. Not much, but there had been four people in the bunks. The personal effects were under the bunks. He would have to go through all that carefully. They would have to learn who the two skeletons were. That would leave the killers identified.

The captain's quarters. There was a listing of log dates that ended thirty five years ago. Clint glanced at some entries and smirked.

September 9, 1977: I am much confused. This isn't the Bahamas. We are standing offshore of some islands, but they are not occupied except by strange people. They are not like the Indians in the Caribbean. They are like the Danes. They do not speak Danish though I recognized several words. They are large and muscular people and are living as savages. They are threatening and dangerous. We will sail from here toward the south and move on toward the Panama Canal.

There is civilization there at least. Our locator equipment is useless. I think that lightning strike has burned out all of it. The radio gets only static. I tried to use the old star locator last night but the stars don't seem to be in the same places. Our food is very low now. George is ill. Ahmad is terrified of the unknown. He keeps saying Allah is not in this place. We are lost to the gods. I begin to wonder if that is not true. There is nothing here that I remember. I have been here twice before. We saw a sea monster a huge ugly thing. I fear we truly are lost.

Clint sighed. Thirty six years ago? The ink wasn't more than a few weeks old.

He took the log and the bill of lading. The ship was supposedly carrying 50 plastic drums of maple syrup and a lot of farming equipment. The syrup was to go to New Orleans, Louisiana. The farm equipment was to go to Galveston, Texas. The misc. was to go to Mexico? Misc.?

Clint checked the insurance. It only listed misc. household furniture. Used.

Value of only $200.00? That half a hold full of things covered with tarps was used household furniture worth two hundred bucks?

He went through the papers, then to the ledger. The cost of delivering two hundred dollars worth of used household furniture was eight thousand five hundred dollars?

Clint went to the forward hold. The household furniture was supposed to be there. He moved the tarps and found some – used furniture. Solid oak and good quality, but household furniture.

Okay. Declared value, two hundred bucks. No import taxes.

There had to be more than that!

He slid open a drawer in a chest of drawers. Old clothes were left in the furniture?

He took out a pair of blue jeans with fading and knees worn through like in the ... so. This was designer stuff that was both popular and very expensive in the mid-seventies!

He slid open another drawer. Empty. Another. Empty. The bottom drawer. Empty, but with a heavy scar in the bottom.

He went to another large chest of drawers. There were only a few shirts. Tie-dyed. Not much value.

A Cedar Chest. It would be worth a couple of thousand. It was old and in perfect condition.

It was scarred inside. There was an old rag that smelled of ... naptha? Gun oil?

Several other items had scars in the bottom. Some smelled of gun oil.

So. Guns were the real cargo then. To Mexico, where they were then sent to little revolutions in Central and South America? What happened?

Why go through this now? What had happened that would make it necessary that the ship turn up?

He went to the center hold. Drums of syrup. Was that what was in them?

He opened one. Maple syrup. Maybe only the forward hold carried guns. The syrup on today's market would be about six times what it was in seventy six.

He went to the popa hold. Boxes of farming equipment. That seemed legitimate.

He moved among the boxes and found another skeleton, this one with a uniform with "Ahmad" on the name tag.

There was something on that boat that made it necessary that it be found. What could it be?

Tonio came to say the boat was coming to take the body and two skeletons to Chiriqui Grande for identification. Clint showed him the third skeleton.

"So the last one will be the killer and who was the inside man. What happened out there?" Tonio asked.

"I think maybe someone found that the cargo wasn't what was on the manifest and that they either tried to get a cut or were going to let the cat out of the bag."

"Speaking of which, we found Lizeth's cat. It's

in the wheelhouse and seems to think the boat belongs to it!"

"It does if it's in the will. This ship was carrying contraband weapons in the household furniture to be delivered to Mexico. I've learned that much!"

"Then what happened? Why bring it here thirty five years later?"

"That's what has me wondering. There has to be something else. There has to be a reason this boat's here now. It's not to have us discover it carried weapons – I don't ... maybe it is! Maybe the big question is *who* was selling or buying those weapons!

"That doesn't make a lot of sense, but it makes some. We don't have anything else. Anonymity would be why it was done this way. The skeleton that's not here was the inside man. Maybe he still is!"

"He's trying to protect someone. Whoever was dealing in contraband weapons is in a position where his involvement must not be known.

"Why Panamá?"

"Seventy five or six. Who was the big shot here then? Who was ... Venezuela?"

"Revolutions and drug wars in Colombia?"

"Panamá and Venezuela were on good terms then. Oil? There was a huge stink about then about oil, I seem to remember."

"We're wasting time speculating. If we find who was dealing, we'll know what else there is."

"It has to be big. That captain and the surviving crewman were somewhere with this ship close. It was someplace the ship wouldn't be noted, which would mean a scrap yard or drydock, probably in Mexico. Maybe Guatemala or Belize. I don't think Honduras ... Nicaragua? The bunch in power now? It will tell us who financed ... no. That was later, but may have been in the planning stages.

"As you say, we'll have to find out who was dealing weapons. To do that we'll have to have that fourth crew member. He's managed to stay anonymous for thirty six years. It won't be an easy task."

"Clint, the fact the US Coast Guard didn't find this ship says something to me."

"I was thinking along those lines. Colón? There are a lot of places there where a ship like this wouldn't be noticed. It would come close to the shore to here to avoid being noted by the coast guard. Inside the limit."

"And it would have to have passed close to Cusapín."

"And along the coast of the comarca. The coast guard won't have noted it's passing, but my people would!"

"We can find who the crew members were from

the log records in the captain's cabin. They were both wearing shorts that may have an identifying mark or something. All those clothes are marked on a ship where they have a shared bunk room. We already know the names of all of them."

"Which are? We know this one was Ahmad Something."

"Ahmad Khava, Lebanese. George Earl Fields, gringo. Leon Vargas, Dominican. Sean Kelly, Ireland."

"Kelly might be on the arms end. IRA."

"Doc checked everything. Maybe he saw a mark and can tell us who the others are. He would put it on his report, but we can use the information now." He took his cellular out and called Cortez, who said one pair had SK in marker ink and the other had LV.

"So the gringo is who we're looking for. George Earl Fields."

"It would seem."

They went up on deck. Clint put the log and register in his satchel with all the other papers. He would study them back at the station.

Lizeth said she wasn't any use there and would go back to Chiriqui Grande with Clint. Esteban would stay aboard to keep watch on the ship. Tonio would go back with Clint.

They tied to the dock and Lizeth went to the

aduana station while Clint and Tonio went to the station to study those papers. Clint hoped there would be a name for who sold those weapons. It could lead to some very interesting things. He also wanted to find a way to trace George Earl Fields – and he just might have that!

He called Manolo, a friend who worked with Interpol, et al. He had contacts in Colón who could find anything.

Tonio and Clint had a good lunch in the little restaurant by the public docks, then went to the station.

"I've read a little on the log. It was supposed to have been written thirty years ago, but the ink is fresh. Thirty days, maybe," Clint reported. "He was trying to make it sound like they were caught in a dimensional or time warp. It reads like some of those SciFi things.

"That was to, hopefully, make us think we had an explanation, if a weird one, for the ship being here. He used the fuel he had figured to the meter to put him there when it ran out. He was probably in the engine room to exhaust the batteries, which he did when he was hit over the head.

"We have all these papers. I think the log ... will be phony from the start of the trip if not before.

"We have the bill of lading. Part of it is false. Part legitimate. There may be something there to give a hint."

Tonio was looking at one of the bills of lading. "This is for Sweet North Maple Products. Fifty fifty five gallon drums of pure maple syrup for Allstate Distributors in New Orleans."

"This one is for the farm equipment list. Manning Transporters. It's legit, I'd say.

"This is for the furniture. Bayside Refurbishers. Richmond, Virginia.

"Uh-oh!"

"Uh-oh?"

"Richmond. FBI headquarters."

"So. This could be a CIA operation that was designed to aid some little revolution that would backfire and smack the US government in the face like all those drugs for arms deals?"

"I don't like this! I have to get my hands on Fields. If it's that, the US government is having people killed who might expose what they were doing. I have to check something."

He called Manolo and said he wanted to know if Fields was CIA.

"Another deal they made turned back on them?"

"I think it's a lot more possible than I want to believe."

"That gives me a little more of a way to locate him. I already have one person who's checking to see if someone he's been suspicious of has been there for the past few days."

They chatted a bit longer, then Clint went back to the papers. There wasn't much more.

He went to the computer to check on Bayside Refurbishers. It was a small company that had been licensed for eight years before this deal. It had gone out of business when the owner, Daniel

Grant, died, leaving it to a daughter who didn't care to continue it and couldn't sell it.

He checked on Daniel Grant. He seemed to be a legitimate shop owner. It didn't have the smell of the government agencies.

He had a daughter, Isabel, who was married to a state senator, Felix Fernando Falconer, at the time of his death.

He checked F. F. Falconer. He was a typical type of politician. He had practiced banking law until he got in with the Republican Party in the state and was personable and clean enough that they were pushing him to higher office. There was talk of running him for VP the next election. He was being groomed to shoot for the top.

"I may have found something. If Falconer was part of that company he could have set up the deal with the guns. He was a lawyer then with a big banking firm. He's been in politics for sixteen years. He's supposed to be squeaky clean and is being groomed to run for president in a few years. He's for strong banking laws, yet they back him. They say he's fair.

"Someone doesn't think he's the best selection, it would seem."

"If they can connect him with gunrunning, he won't seem quite so squeaky clean," Tonio said. "I don't care. I have a murder in my province to solve. The politicians can cover their part up, probably, but I'm not so easy to use. The murder will be prosecuted. Any interference by a foreign government will be noted in the international press. If they try to cover it up by manipulating the courts here they'll find that was the wrong path to follow!"

"I don't know. Maybe a new house and car and yacht and private jet and that sort of thing?"

"If I want any of that, I can ask you and you'll buy it for me."

Clint gave him the finger. He picked up the ledger. It had records of the transaction made for a number of trips. It had check numbers and cash transfers recorded in fine detail.

Clint went through several dozen records. He couldn't find anything except the maple syrup. The cash transfers were the method used with the farm equipment. There was nothing about the furniture except "dfod".

"You have to find out what that means!" Tonio declared.

He went through other transactions and found the "dfod" notation on one.

He shook his head and picked up the delivery receipts. He found the first "dfod" and noted it was paid on delivery. He thought for a minute and checked the log. He remembered seeing something about a payment on delivery. It took him four or five minutes to find: *contract for deferred payment on delivery.*

"It means paid on delivery."

He found the delivery note for the furniture.

Delivery note? It was still there!

But it was paid. By bank check drawn on the Bank of Mexico. He had the check number, but didn't have a prayer of getting any information on it from Mexico.

He remembered something else! He had needed information on another case where Mexico was used by some people who wanted to transport uranium.

He called Manny Matthews, actually Marko Bocinni, head of one of the most powerful mafia organizations in the US. Clint had helped him set up the new ID as Manny Matthews. He lived with his family on Isla San Cristóbal. He helped Clint several times in cases.

He gave Manny the check number. Ten minutes later he got the call back that it was sold to Frank F. Fontaine from the US through his personal representative, Earl Fielding.

Wow! Talk about coincidental initial matches and such things!

"It's a matter of proving it and seeing what's really behind it," Tonio said. "I don't see it. All they had to do was nothing. There has to be more behind it than this. It was thirty six years ago. If someone wanted to stop us finding that ship all they had to do was knock off Garcia before he took it out."

"Which tells me Garcia had something else or some other motive."

"Fields can give us that."

"I hope!"

Manolo called a few minutes later to say, "Clint, Fields isn't CIA. He was gone from Colón for a week or so, but got back yesterday. He's using the name of Francis Fielding. He's working covertly for the offshore banking industry. His father was Fielding, his mother was Isaacs. There are a lot of spaces in his resume if I might be poetic."

"You might, but not that time.

"What? We're into conspiracy now?"

"Not too deep, but that could change with new information. He's definitely in with the really big money and the world bank idea. I don't know what else he's into."

"He's into murder. That's my field."

"Well, tag him for it and see who runs to his defense. Have you found anything else about it?"

"A cheap politician who was in on contraband weapons deals and who's being groomed to run for president a few years down the road. Fields works for him. I don't know which job's on the side."

"Fields' type? They're all on the side."

"Could be. Highest bidder. Somebody bids to have you knocked off and offers more than you do, you get knocked off."

They soon rang off. Clint sat thinking for a few minutes, then said he was going to have to go to Colón. What a thrill!

He called his wife and said he would be there by dark, but would have to leave again in the morning. He was going to Colón.

He told Tonio he would be back early in the morning and would go to David to catch a flight to Colón. He was going to use a disguise. James Hanrady rides again!

The somewhat out of shape person who looked a lot like Clint Faraday got off the plane and looked around. This was reputed to be a very dangerous place, but he could take care of himself.

He hailed a taxi and said to take him to the Inlandia Hotel. The driver said, "Ten balboas!"

"Fuck you. One fifty. I'm Panamanian. I just look like a gringo."

The driver grinned and took him the kilometer to the hotel. He got out and went in to say he had a reservation. James Hanrady.

Fields or Fielding or whatever was staying at the hotel. He was a resident there, having a yearly lease on the place.

He was shown to his room. It was standard for the type of hotel. He cleaned up and went to the restaurant to order an early lunch. The service was what he would call surly, so he responded in kind.

A man came to the door to look around. Clint chose that moment to tap his menu three times with his index finger.

Manolo walked by the table and on. There was a slip on the table. Clint read it and ignored it. It was a phone number.

Clint waited a few minutes and acted like he was getting mad about something. He finally took out his cheap throwaway cellular and punched a number. Manolo answered.

"Is Evelyn there?" Clint demanded just loud enough for the waitress to hear.

"Yeah, Sweetums. What you want, Doll? Fifty dollars!" Manolo answered.

"Well, where the hell is she? She was supposed to be here fifteen minutes ago!"

"He's at the container dock. He seems to be waiting for something."

"Like, when will she be back?"

"He might be there awhile. Whatever he's

waiting for isn't there yet."

"Well, tell her to fuck off! There's something better on any street corner here!"

"You really aren't my type. I was only after the money, Hotsums!"

Clint cut the phone off and dropped it into his pocket. He looked at the menu and made a face. He got up and walked out. The waitress didn't seem to notice.

Clint got into a taxi and said to take him to Containers International Delivery.

"Ten dollars."

"Go fuck yourself! Two fifty."

"Okay."

He got off at the office on the street by the entrance to the docks. A man he'd met in David was there, a big black with a big diamond ring and a cigar. He took that moment to scratch his left ear. Clint looked at the watch he wasn't wearing. The man turned to spit toward the end dockage where a container ship was unloading.

Amos worked with Manolo at times. Clint went along the rail toward the ship. A big blond man of about fifty five years was standing there checking the code numbers on each container as it was offloaded. Clint asked him if number fifteen fifteen ten A was unloaded yet.

"Nope. Not on this ship. These are all twelve

twenty two numbers today. Fifteen fifteen comes tomorrow." Clint knew that from Manolo. He said, "Shit! Thanks!" and walked off.

Manolo came along the dock. He stopped and said to show a pass or leave. Clint sighed and walked toward the gate as Manolo went to the blond to repeat what he said to Clint. The man swore and said he was only there to receive a container from that ship.

"Get a permit from the office. One minute. Wear a hard hat."

The man came toward the gate. Clint said that was a new one on him!

"It's the rules. They usually don't say anything, but have to when the inspectors are around."

"You're Fieldinghouse, aren't you? We met in Mexico City a few years ago. I'm Jim Hanrady."

"Just Fielding. I haven't been to Mexico City for six years!"

"Yes. It was about then. You meet people in the strangest places! I never forget a face. I never remember a name."

"Well, I'd better get a permit. My luck they'll unload the damned thing and put it under nine others to make it almost impossible to dig out later."

Clint waved and went out the gate. He turned left and Fielding turned right.

Clint turned around and called, "Is your boss here? That Falconright fellow?"

"Er! Uh! No, he's back in the states. I haven't seen him since Mexico City."

Clint waved and went on.

So. Falconer had been in Mexico City six years ago with Fielding. Interesting!

Now to manufacture a chat with Fielding.

Manolo said it would be easy enough to get to chat with Fielding in Colón. They would set something up. There was nothing important in that container. Just things he was supposed to see were shipped on.

"Okay. Here's how we'll handle it. You know Tiburón Carlos? From Bocas?"

"Big black? Mean looking as hell, but no spine? Glass jaw?"

"That pretty well describes him. All bluff and bravado.

"Fielding always goes to the apartment of a girl four blocks from the hotel. He's big enough that he doesn't get too much concerned about walking home. A lot of people here know him.

"He'll leave her apartment about eleven. Carlos will be there with...."

Fielding looked up and down the street, then came out of the steel door to the stairs at Sylvia's apartment and walked down to the first corner, turned right and went two blocks, then turned left, a block from the hotel. He was almost to the hotel when a really mean-looking big black grabbed the back of his shirt and yanked him into the little alley. He put a knife to his throat and said, "Make a noise and it'll be your last! You got no money, say bye-bye to this world!"

That Jim Hanrady person stepped into the alley behind the big black, who didn't see him there. Hanrady produced a mean little pistol from somewhere, stuck it in the black's ear, and said, "You're the one who's going bye-bye! Drop the shiv or I drop you!"

He dropped the knife. Hanrady kicked it out onto the sidewalk and said, "This a private beef I'm sticking my nose into or does this turkey buy it right here?" to Fielding.

"Hey, man! It was a joke! I only like to scare gringos! I wouldn't hurt him!"

"Not if he gave you some money."

"It was just a joke!" Carlos whined.

"Take a fucking hike! I ever see you again I might just waste you on general principles!"

"Can I get my knife, Man? It cost twenty two dollars!"

"Yeah, yeah. Keep it in your pocket."

Carlos grabbed the knife and ran down the street.

"I was coming out of the hotel and saw you get yanked into this alley. I didn't have anything else to do so I decided to keep you from getting your throat cut.

"Don't go anywhere alone at night here. It can get hairy!"

"I live here part time! This is the first time anyone's tried anything with me!"

"I haven't been here for a year or more. I don't like the place. Too much shit like that.

"I saved your life. Buy me a drink?"

"Ten! Lead on!"

They went into the hotel bar and Clint ordered a tequila and beer. They went to a little table and sat.

"You don't look like the type who would face that big ugly pig," Fielding said. "I think maybe you've been around. You were in Mexico City. Do you work for those bankers too?"

"Bankers? When hell freezes over!"

"Who?"

"Myself, mostly. I'm what you might call an independent contractor. I'm an engineer by trade, but that's a boring life. Or non-life."

"Yeah. I've had some good times. Jobs with a little adrenalin rush in them. I just get by with things like seeing that transfers go within six months of the schedule. Time doesn't mean the same thing here as everywhere else."

"Been here long?"

"I was here thirty some-odd years ago. Brought in a cargo ship from the states. I think that was an insurance fraud deal, but I got paid. I don't care if some big insurance company gets ripped off. It doesn't happen often enough. They lose a cargo for a million and raise the rates worldwide fifty bucks a load to compensate for their huge loss, meaning they make fifty million because of it. Makes you sick!"

"It's the same bunch of bankers and politicians you were working for in Mexico City. I was working for a, shall we say, competing factor. They have the world so fucked up it won't ever recover. I'm glad I'm now and not in twenty years!"

"Yeah. That's why I came back. When I was here before I really liked the place, but it's a lot different now. Back then they were just getting into the drug thing. That turned it sour. I thought at first they were going to change the numbers on the ship and use it for that, but it's not the kind of thing they could get away with."

"No. Better to scuttle the thing after you take off the cargo to put on the second market."

"I suggested that. They took it somewhere and stored it, I think. It'll be a lump of rust in one of the bays around here. There have to be five hundred of them.

"It's sort of weird. Use me to get the damned thing, then hide if from me. Like I give a shit, but some of my stuff was on it. They could have at least given me that crap.

"What the hell! I got paid enough to buy some new clothes. Fuck it!"

"So? Why come back here? There're a lot of better places in Panamá than Colón! Almost anywhere is better in today's world."

"I can get work here. I've been here nine years, but mostly in the city. I went to Bocas first, but that's got too many people who might ... let's just say I didn't want to take any chances of being identified. There are people who would like to see me disappear forever. They've got the power, baby!"

"How do you know I'm not one of them?"

"They want me dead. You saved my life."

"Ah, that one would just cut you a little. He wouldn't kill a gringo in a place like that. Maybe out on the road, but not that close to anything. You give him twenty bucks and he walks away."

"It would be the same thing. I'd end up in a hospital. I wouldn't have any valid ID and they'd end up notifying the states, those people would know in ten minutes, I'd be dead in an hour. The way I operate only works here. They don't question an ID with ... of a certain type. I stay in the apartment a little, but most of my time's on the bay. At Lagarteria. Nobody could care less there.”

“Like this crap?” Clint handed him an official-looking card that said he was Bill Jones, from Sydney, Australia.

“Very good work! Better than mine in some ways. How much did it cost you?”

“A buck and a quarter to put it in plastic. I ran it off on my handy-dandy laptop.”

“Shit! This thing cost me eight hundred!”

“Well, cheers! and all that!” Clint swallowed the shot of tequila, stood and went to the elevator. He hadn’t swallowed the story Fielding gave him there, but he did learn a lot of what he wanted to know. When combined with the dock few words it gave him an answer. He knew how he wanted a press release worded. He headed back to Chiriqui Grande in the morning.

“He has a prepared story. He has all the props ready to use. I doubt he tumbled on me, but he’s not about to take chances.”

“Now it looks like CIA,” Tonio suggested.

“Yeah, but it’s not. It’s just set up by that same crowd with the same mentality behind it.”

“Politics and big money. I agree.

“Have you discovered what that ship’s about?”

“I can guess. He let the cat out of the bag there when I said I was on the opposing side in Mexico

City."

"He did?"

"That's what the opposition would do."

"You aren't making any sense agai ... which told you there *is* an opposition. I see. The reaction he didn't give told you a great deal more than what he was saying."

"As the wise old saying goes, Bingo!"

"So? What now? You're just playing games. We put him on the boat and my part's done. We have to find where the boat was kept and why those skeletons were still on it. I could see why they'd put them on it when they brought it here, but Doc says they were where they died. Thirty five years ago or more.

"Khava was shot in the head. He doesn't know what killed the other two."

"The ship was in one of those hundreds of deepwater lagoons near Lagartria. He's been staying there for about eight or nine years. O want to know what happened then that made them send him to find the boat? Garcia probably had a place to leave the boat and he probably was going to sell the cargo on the black market, but they had paid him enough to park the thing there and walk away. Something happened nine years ago that caused them to want that boat accounted for in a way ... I'll be damned! I'll bet that's it!

"Tonio, I now have to find out where Garcia was staying and what happened with him! Someone didn't come back home and the answers are there! I need the canal records from ... I guess thirty five years ago means we won't get them."

"No. The US coast guard wasn't involved except for the trade ships and tankers and such. What do you need, really?

"There will be a note that Garcia brought a ship in. Not in the canal, except perhaps at Gatún. They would have a little note that such-and-such a ship passed into the lake. Back then they could have gone ... Clint, they could have put on false numbers and flags back then. There wasn't any concentration about drugs or anything. There are repair and drydock, innocent ones, around that Lago. Register that the thing is from Timbuktu in for repairs. A note on a ledger. Never read again.

"It was easy then. We can, in this limited case, assume."

"So we have to know what happened ten years ago that made that boat a factor after all those years. It will hinge primarily on Garcia if what I'm thinking happened."

"What happened?"

"He spent all the money. His papers were false. He could never captain a ship again. It's all he knew."

"We have information requests out in the places you suggested," Tonio said. "Most of them have replied that he wasn't there."

"I think there are a limited number of places he could have been. He'd want the ocean, a place where there's at least moderate access to good restaurants and bars."

"You've considered the islands? Isla Taboga?"

"I'm thinking Isla del Rey. San Miguel. It fits everything, is big money, no real questions."

Tonio thought for a minute. "Yes. He'll want night life. The Chiriqui islands don't have what he'd want. They do have some shore towns. Las Tablas, Chitré, Mariato, San Carlos."

"They're checked. I think it's going to be Isla del Rey. San Miguel or very close.

"Let's get a press release that says things in a certain way."

Tonio called in a secretary to take a story Clint would give him for release to the press.

"We want it to look like a strange happening with certain inconsistencies," Clint explained. "Here are a few suggestions...."

Chiriqui Grande:

A ship was found sitting in the harbor mouth at Chiriqui Grande for three days. The police and aduana investigated to find it is a ship that disappeared from what is called the Devil's Triangle north of the Bahamas in 1976.

The ship was not noted by either Panamanian authorities nor EE. UU. Coast Guard surveillance.

The ship seemed deserted. Aduana and Police Jefe Tonio Serrano boarded the vessel in the company of Clinton Faraday, who is known for assisting the police in many matters.

There were three skeletons that the medical examiner determined had been dead since the approximate time the ship first disappeared. This began to appear to be another of those strange paranormal happening from the Devil's Triangle. The ship's fuel tanks were totally exhausted and the batteries were same.

The investigation then found the body of the captain of the Liberian registered vessel, Capitan Enrique Garcia of Dominica, in the engine room. He had been dead but a few hours.

"That sort of put an end to the idea of another paranormal event," Sr. Faraday said. "It also tells us that someone else was aboard the boat. Garcia was murdered by a solid being, not by any

ghost."

The investigation will continue until resolution.

"Pretty much what I wanted," Clint said as they watched the news on television. "It'll let someone know whatever they planned fell apart. I think Fielding will have another job, but ... we can watch him! He'll know the only other loose end now is where Garcia was living!"

"Yes. He can lead us to the place, though Goldez says he was staying in a leased house in San Miguel. I've ordered the place sealed until you investigate. The helicopter will be here in about half an hour to take you there. I knew you would want that."

Clint nodded and went to his boat to get a few things, then called Tyna to explain. She was used to him having to be away a lot and said to be careful.

He got on the chopper as soon as it was there and was headed for the big island off the coast near Panamá City. The island was big money. He would have to watch out for the politicians there. This was tied to politicians in the states. It would as much as automatically be nasty and dirty.

He was put off on the little chopper field behind the police station and went inside. Goldez was assigned to accompany him to the semi-ritzy big house on the coast with the blue tile roof.

The live-in housekeeper was waiting and was indignant that the common police would dare to invade her house! General Francina, rtd. was a respected and admired pillar of the community who had never had any suspicion of any kind against him by the police and there were going to be repercussions so be ready to start looking for other employment.

"He didn't dare to become involved with the police. We would have known from that moment that he was not a general, his name was not Francina and he was in this country illegally," Goldez told her. "We know it now."

"Well, he's not here! I don't believe you!"

"No, he's dead," Clint said. "His name was Garcia. You might have seen something about it on television. Chiriqui Grande.

"Quite frankly, I couldn't care less what you do or don't believe."

"Dios mio! That man! He ... he was from that side! He ... what...?"

"What man?" Goldez said quickly.

"He said his name was Fairchild and that he knew The General from the war in nineteen seventy seven! That he had been in a battle with him and wanted to see him once more before he died! The General left with him. They were going to visit the place where they first came to Panamá for old time's sake! It wasn't Chiriqui Grande, it was Colón!"

"When was this? They had left the ship near there," Clint said. "What did he look like."

She described Fielding. That solidified Tonio's murder case. He could order Fielding arrested and transferred to Chiriqui Grande. Clint called him and told him they would get a declaration from the woman. Dona Arrends. It seemed Garcia trusted the wrong person.

They went into the sealed house. Clint went immediately to the den to locate the hidden wall safe he knew would be there behind a painting. 1970's mentality. He would find the combination somewhere.

He found it in the desk. A ledger of household expenses with dates. Third entry on page three. *Chair, den. $42.50 4-19-09.*

The entry before was on 5-15-10 and after was 5-22-10.

L4 R14 L9 opened the thing. There wasn't much in the safe other than a ledger that showed regular payments of $1,250 every month. From acct. # 107937224677, Bank of Warmington. Clint had an idea that was going to prove a very important number to have

There was a notation at the top of the third page. Garcia seemed to have a fixation on 3. BoP 2313 suc 31.

"What did you learn so far?" Goldez asked.

"I have to find a key and I have to trace a bank account in the states."

"There are a lot of keys in the desk. A little jar of them."

Clint went through the keys. There were two possibilities. He told Goldez they would now have to go to the Bank of Panamá, sucursal thirty one.

"Banco Nacional? I think thirty one would be in the city."

"No. The Bank of Panamá. It's just a few small banks. I've run across them before."

Goldez made a call. "Thirty one is in La Guinea. Forty minutes."

"Let's go!"

"We haven't searched but this room!"

"We found what we were after. Why spend hours looking through the rest ourselves? Get a team here to do the rest of it."

They got a car and headed into the interior of the island. La Guinea was a small town in the area where there were some farms. The bank was closed, but Goldez found the manager and gave him a court order they had made out in San Miguel. The manager went with them to the security boxes. 2313 opened with the first key. There were thirty hundred dollar bills and a shipping manifest. Clint read it over and smirked.

"Damned fool signed his name to the manifest! Shall we go destroy a cheap politician's career?"

"That sounds like fun!"

They went back to San Miguel. Clint downloaded the pictures he'd taken of everything they did and signed out the copies of the evidence of the ledger and the manifest. He headed back to Chiriqui Grande, getting there as it was getting dark. He called his wife and told her he was back and he got what he went for.

"Fielding will be here at ten thirty tomorrow morning," Tonio reported. "He's pulling that confused innocence act. He claimed he was never anywhere near here and didn't know what the hell he was supposed to know about any Capitan Garcia. I'll wait until he's here to ask him why his fingerprints are in that boat and why he went to Garcia's place in Isla Rey and that kind of thing."

"His fingerprints are in the boat? He'll claim they were there for thirty five years ... which would still convict him."

"Fingerprints don't survive five years in those conditions, much less thirty five. As you say, he would still have to explain why he told us he didn't know Garcia and why he took him to Colón and a few little oddities like that. Maybe he could explain why his fingerprints match those of somebody named Fields from a passport that was issued thirty nine years ago. A few little discrepancies in his story that tend to make us suspicious."

Clint laughed. "I reckon!"

Clint went to the little restaurant near the public dock, then to the hotel to clean up, then to the little bar where he chatted with his friends until a little after eleven, then he sacked out.

In the morning he ran to Cusapín to check out the place and deliver some supplies. Tyna and he spent a bit of time together, he caught up on the gossip, got the report on how his kids were doing, then was back in Chiriqui Grande at a little after twelve. Fielding was in the jail where Clint would go after a light lunch. He went to the hotel to change and clean up a bit. When he went back to the lobby, a gringo was there. He asked if he was speaking with the famous Clint Faraday.

"Infamous, but that's me!"

"I'm John Smith from Washington. Could I have a word?"

"Washington? Really? Close to Richmond?"

"I was told I couldn't fool you for ten minutes. Less than one. Pretty good!

"Can I have a word?"

"Have eight or ten. They're small."

"I can see we're not going to get along."

"I have to get over to the police station. Will whatever you want wait?" Clint asked "John Smith."

"It's about what you have to go to the police station for. I don't know what tales he's telling you about things, but he's here hiding from the US Government. I want to assure you what he says doesn't have much in the way of truth attached to it."

"He committed a murder here. On that boat sitting right out there. We have him cold. Why would we believe what he says to try to get out of that noose?"

"Because of another person. A person the dead man worked for at times."

"Which dead man?"

"Er?"

"You said he worked for the dead man. There were four."

"Uh, Captain Garcia."

"Why would we care?"

"Because Garcia was living ... do you know a James Hanrady?"

"Jim? He's a cousin. I've met him face-to-face two times. He's an engineer for some companies or something. Mining engineer. Consultant."

"Did you know that he went to del Rey to investigate this case?"

"Where the hell is del Rey? He wouldn't have anything to do with this case unless someone he worked for wanted information. I can't think of why they would. What's it got to do with me?"

"Oh? Where did you go in the helicopter, Mr. Faraday?"

"None of your fucking business, but Capira. Why?"

"Because a helicopter delivered Hanrady to San Miguel. Isla del Rey. Hanrady went with the police to Garcia's place there and searched for a very short time, then went somewhere in a police car. Hanrady returned and the helicopter flew him out."

"Really? I wonder ... you say where Garcia lived? Garcia's place?"

"Yes. My boss ... the CIA wants to know what he found. Fields was arrested immediately. We have to know what caused that."

"He was seen in Colón with Captain Garcia. His fingerprints are all over several parts of that ship. Garcia's body was on that ship. Two and two is four, believe it or not!"

"The CIA has to know what Hanrady found! It's very important because of, uh, drug smuggling."

"How in hell would you know what the CIA wants? Drug smuggling thirty six years ago? I don't think so! Not on that slow rustbucket!

"I'd really like to listen to a few more tall tales, but I have to go to the station."

"You'd better watch your back, Faraday! You don't know who you're dealing with!"

Something said a fairly long time ago, or so it seemed, occurred to Clint. "Those bankers? You? I'm so scared!" He turned around and headed for the police station.

"What do you know about bankers, Faraday!?" Smith yelled.

"More than I want to. Talk to you later. Maybe. Maybe not."

He went to the station. Tonio was waiting with Fields sitting in a chair looking smug. Before Clint could say anything, Fields said, "You look a hell of a lot like your cousin."

"So I'm told. Want to talk or want to sit there like a log while we send your ass away for about twenty years, which you won't survive."

"I'll be out of here in another hour. There's someone here to see to it."

"John Smith? Did he really fool you? He just wants to know what you might know about some politician or banker or maybe both. I suppose he's got orders he's to silence you in any way possible. People you've worked for don't like to take chances. It's not what you know, it's what they think you know. If we hadn't picked you up, they'd let you ride on it. Now you could be an embarrassment."

He didn't look so smug all of a sudden. "Uh, he's not CIA?"

"Hell no! As fucked up as they are, he's worse. He can't say two lines that don't give him away. They have *some* training in that!"

"Christ! You don't know who you can trust anymore!"

"Nobody can trust you, yet you gripe because you can't trust them? Really?"

He shrugged.

"What's it about?"

"Nothing anyone can do anything about."

"In the long run, maybe. We can do a little bit in the short term and maybe somebody somewhere with half a brain and a little power will figure it out."

"They always have a set of backups. Knock one out and they have two to take it's place."

"Garcia was blackmailing someone?"

"I think so. I didn't ask why. He trusted me from 'way back, so it was easy. I think bringing that ship here was a big mistake. They could have contained it if that thing didn't end up sitting out there."

"You crewed it with him all the way from the lake. You could have ended it anywhere."

"No I didn't! He brought that old derelict up here by himself! I thought I'd talked him out of doing anything stupid and he gave me the slip. They saw it go through the canal mouth and reported it to ... someone. I was called and told to stop it, but I couldn't find it until it passed a few miles out. I got a cayuca and went out to it as soon as he dropped anchor. He was in the engine room and I smacked him, then got back out.

"That boat was just like when I left. Ahmad, Leo and Sean were laying right where they fell.

"See, I helped him with Leo and Sean. So did Ahmad. We were going to dump them overboard and sell the cargo. I went up to check whether that would be a good place to dump them. It wasn't. There were a lot of boats just outside.

"I went down to tell Garcia it was a bad idea. He was in the hold, looking for Ahmad, who was hiding in the drums. He got a shot. He was good. Ahmad was no problem anymore.

"I knew at that moment that I was next. He didn't have a hint of a plan to split anything with me!

"I went over the side in the dory and got out of there. He went on to the mouth and through. He had pasted some phony numbers over the real ones. He radioed earlier that we were coming through for repairs.

"I didn't know where he put the damned ship. He had a good place picked out. He'd been there before. I think he ran it into a cove or something and just left it. Maybe a drydock or storage. By the looks of it, that thing hadn't been touched since the night he took it in to wherever he left it. He had some kind of deal with someone.

"See, I figured if he had a deal with someone, it wouldn't be much of a good idea to be around. I went out through Costa Rica and got into some people in the states. I went to Mexico City and Hong Kong and Australia and everywhere, then came here to sort of retire.

"I didn't know that the people who backed him were the people I was working for. They kept me shut up by acting like I just happened and fit what they needed. He tried to pull something and took that boat down here. They called me and said they knew all about everything and always had, that I took care of Garcia or they would take care of me. I'm to be paid half a mil for it.

"That's what I know! You're right! They have to shut me up!"

"We can protect you," Tonio said. "You still get the murder rap. Maybe you aren't interested in being protected?"

"I'll try to stay around just to see what happens. What do I do now?"

Tonio had him make a concise statement, then arranged for him to be sent to a small place between Chiriqui Grande and David where no one would look for him.

"He'll manage to escape. Should I stop him?" Tonio asked.

"No. He can kill off all of that type he wants. You solved the case from your end. I still have to do a few things from mine. No need for us to have to feed and house him for twenty years! I doubt he'll get far."

"What now for you?"

"I have to find a way to make a cheap crooked politician lose an election a few years down the line."

"Good luck!"

Clint went back out. Smith was waiting to ask what happened.

"It's none of your fucking business. We caught a murderer, he'll get convicted. I'll go home to my wife and kids and wait for the next idiot who thinks he can shut something up by killing off people."

"You don't want to know what he was doing? What Garcia had?"

"Garcia was into blackmailing someone in the states. Why should we give a fuck? Do you know the percent of blackmailers who end up killed?"

"Fields doesn't have that evidence?"

"How in hell would he?"

"He went to del Rey and went with Garcia to Colón. He could have something passed into his hands for safekeeping."

"By Garcia? Fat chance! When Garcia knew full-well he couldn't trust Fields?"

"Then Hanrady must have gotten it. That's the only reason the man in the police there wouldn't know about it."

"Maybe there wasn't any evidence? Maybe it was all bluff?"

"He had the evidence. There's a copy."

"Then what the hell is the point of knocking off Garcia?"

"The evidence doesn't mean anything without the connection. Garcia was the connection."

And that ship is the other connection! Clint thought. He shrugged.

"Then the connection's already broken. Why worry about Fields?"

"We don't have to worry about it if he doesn't have anything. Garcia's still the connection if he does."

"You know what it is? You think if Fields is out of the equation no one else can bring it up?"

"It's a piece of paper is all I know. Only Fields can connect it with a certain person now. Without Garcia's name definitely connected it doesn't mean anything."

"So Fields will bring pressure to get out of the rap. The deal will be that he gets off, you get the paper."

"Something like that."

"So Cousin Jim can't do anything, even if he has the paper?"

"He has a piece of paper. He can claim anything he wants, but he can't produce a connection."

"If he has a paper he got from Garcia's place?"

"I hope he does! If he's taken it out of the place he can't prove anything and the issue's dead in the water!"

Clint nodded. The name of the ship was on the manifest he had. Someone was overlooking a very important point!

He had an idea. There may be a damned good reason they didn't know that! Garcia didn't give them all the facts! He had to look at some things!

He told Smith he supposed his job was over if Fields didn't demand protection. If he didn't, he didn't have any paper.

Clint went toward the dock. Smith went back into the hotel. Clint crossed the road and went to the station against the side where he couldn't be seen from the hotel.

Tonio looked up as Clint came rushing in. He asked what the excitement was about.

"I have to see those manifests we got on the ship!"

Tonio shrugged and took him to the evidence room. He went through and took out four of the manifests.

"Shit! I saw it somewhere! These don't say anything ... wasn't there more to the one in the security box?"

Tonio took out the clear plastic bag with the manifest. It had a section on top that wasn't on the other manifests. It was number 3033.

"I see where his fixation on three came from. I have to go back onto the boat. I need the manifest contract pad that was used.

"We brought everything. It'll be in that box right there. Indirect evidence."

Clint went through and took out the pad. There were receipt stubs in it like the top part of the one Tonio had from the security box.

"He hedged his bet. He would have been a lot smarter to let them know it.

"Put this pad into the direct evidence, Tonio!"

Tonio looked at the pad and the manifest. A grin spread across his face. "Apparently your politician forgot he had to sign both bottom and top. He got a copy of the manifest below the tear-off line!"

"Uh-huh! And we don't need Garcia or Fields or anyone else if we have that boat that's sitting right out there!"

"We don't really need that. It merely makes it a bit more solid. It's plenty solid without it!"

The tops of all the pages were still in the book. Numbers 3001-3032 were there. 3033 was missing. 3034 and 3035 were there, then there were no more stubs. The whole manifest page to 3049. 3034 was for maple syrup, signed by Arnold Sampson. 50 drums. 3035 was for farm machinery, 162 boxes, signed by Killian Forest. The name of the boat and registration number were on the top of both sections.

"But why bring that boat here?"Tonio asked.

"Because that furniture is there and the evidence of what was in it is still there. Without that this is only a manifest for used furniture. With it it's concession time!"

"I'm going home to the wife and kids. You do whatever you do. I'll be back on Monday."

"Will do!"

"Ah! Smith! Still around?"

"Oh. Hello, Faraday. What's up?"

"Besides taxes and my blood pressure, not too much. How's with you?"

"Same old shit. I like the country, but there's nothing to do in Chiriqui Grande."

"No reason for you to be here anymore that I can see."

"Me either. They say to hang around for just one more week, then I can go back."

"What happens in a week?"

"An election. One of my bosses is running for attorney general of the state."

"Ah! Now I see! That paper shows he was into gunrunning in the mid-seventies! The statute of limitations doesn't mean shit to things anymore, but it doesn't have anything to do with what people know affecting an election. I knew all along rotten politics had to be behind something. It stunk of them.

"What does that have to do with the bankers?"

Smith grinned and shook his head. "They're grooming him to run for a higher office. He's for a world bank."

"So am I, but only so long as that disgusting crowd controlling things now isn't involved. It's coming. It's just a matter of keeping those toads out of it."

"Can't happen. You're lucky you're living here where it won't have any real effect for fifty years down the line."

"Well, we can try to put it off a year at a time. If getting a politician unelected who's backing them slows things a little when they have to go to candidate 'B' – we can hope!"

"I doubt that can happen here. He'll get elected and have four years to make sure it never comes up."

"Could be! I think they might be in for a big surprise."

"Really? Why?"

"Remember my cousin, Jim? He really did have something, it seems."

"Oh, shit! It will be a minor type of thing he can deny. There's no connection."

"Yes, there is. There's that ship sitting right out there. They didn't pull it away because of it."

"The ship? I don't...?"

"A connection. That ship's on the paper. The proof of the cargo is still on the ship."

"But the manifest could have been for anything.

Another time, another trip."

"No. They have the manifest numbers. It was that ship and that trip and the stuff was taken to the dock by your candidate, where he signed the manifest as soon as it was aboard. The manifest carbon copy was removed from the pad, but the original and stub were left there."

"Stub?"

"Falconer should have remembered that he had to sign both the stub and the manifest. Garcia made the mistake of showing a copy or whatever of the manifest, but he didn't include a copy of the stub, which he had and which Jim now has – or had. I think he turned it over to the embassy with ten witnesses or something. Witnesses from the international press."

"Oh, shit!"

"And Fields escaped. They don't know where he is."

"You don't?"

"I do. The police don't. Jim knows. We don't need him. We don't need to house and feed him for knocking off a gunrunner. He's in Costa Rica or farther by now.

"Relax and enjoy a vacation. Your job's over."

"Maybe I'll do that."

Clint grinned and went to the hotel where Tyna was staying for the night before they went home.

Clint had just come back from Panamá City where he had been James Hanrady, his cousin, again for a press conference at the US Embassy.

Tyna and Clint went to the hotel restaurant. The waitress said Clint's cousin was on the news! They went to where they could see the TV.

"... running back then. He seems to have been backed by certain international figures even the, who wanted money and didn't care how they got it," Hanrady was saying. "It led to four murders back then and one now. The statute of limitations would keep him from being prosecuted for the gunrunning. There is no statute of limitations on murder, not to mention one was only a week or so ago. The person who committed that murder has made a clear declaration that it was paid for by Mr. Falconer.

"We have no hope of ever having Falconer extradited to face charges here from the United States. He must consider the rest of his life before he travels anywhere else. If they have extradition that's more than a joke, he will face charges here.

"There are others implicated. The police will not tender that information. Some of them may someday come to Panamá where they will face charges. It would shock and amaze many people to know who they are!

"My cousin, Clint Faraday, was working with

the police, as he often does. He says he sort of regrets that it wasn't actually a derelict from the Devil's Triangle. That would really be a different kind of case!"

"That was Mr. James Hanrady, speaking from Panamá City, Panamá. CBS News has asked Mr. Falconer to respond to the charges, but he is indisposed at this time. (Knowing smirk.)

"Well, Anita! All I can say is that I'm very glad Falconer isn't from this state!

"CBS News, Denver, will return after these messages."

"That was from Denver?!" Clint cried.

"Yes. We get them on cable. It seems they had a reporter here to get your cousin's statement! That's really exciting, happening here in Chiriqui Grande! The ship's still out there, but Tonio says it'll be towed away tomorrow. Maybe you can talk him into putting it off for a few days? It's good for business! People are coming from all over to take pictures!"

"Oh, it'll be parked there for quite awhile. That was tomorrow, Panamanian, which means sometime in the future," Tyna replied. "I'll have the carne guisada corriente. Clint would probably prefer the chuleta.

"I'm glad things are back to a close to normal as they get for us!"

Clint was too.

C. D. Moulton's works are available on most major outlets as printed or e-books. CD writes the CD Grimes, PI, mysteries, the Det. Lt. Nick Storie mysteries, the Clint Faraday mysteries, the Flight of the Maita science fiction series, books on orchid culture and many others of many types. Mystery, adventure, intrigue, science fiction, humor, fantasy, paranormal, mild erotica, and factual.